# My UNICORN is having a BABY

# This book belongs to

_____

My Unicorn is having a baby!
She looks like she's going to pop!

She can't possibly be comfy,
I hope she doesn't drop!

My Unicorn is getting bigger!
What a special surprise!

Will it be a boy or a girl?
Will it have my Unicorn's eyes?

Will it have a sparkly horn,
Or RAINBOW painted toes?

Can I take it for a walk?
Do I lead it by the nose?

Will it drink from a bottle?

Or straight from the tap?

Will it fall asleep soundly,
Right into my lap?

What will my Unicorn eat?
I don't have a clue!

Will it eat glittery hay,
Colored in pink and blue?

Will it know it's a Unicorn?
Special in every way?


Will it moo, cluck, or bark,
Or will it know how to neigh?

Can I comb its long hair,
And make it soft and lush?

Will it be shiny and smooth,
Will I use a magical hair brush?

How small will it be?
Could it fit in a sack?

Can I take it to school,
Will it fit in my backpack?

Will the Unicorn take a bath?
With lots of bubbles and toys?

Will it jump and run away,
And make a lot of noise?

**Will it play until night?**
**And slide down rainbows each day?**

Or will it sleep under a sparkly tree,
And rest until the next day?

I wonder what they will look like,
Will she have more than one?

I am so excited!
This will be so much fun!

I wonder what it will be like,
When the baby Unicorn is here.

One thing I know for sure,
Is that I will hold it near!

The baby Unicorn is coming!
I can't believe my eyes!

She had a BOY and a GIRL!
What a surprise!

The baby Unicorns are so tiny,
This is so much fun!

I can't wait to play with them,
Our adventure has just begun!

If you enjoyed this magical story, please take a moment to share and review online!

Tag readings, pictures and reviews to @Littleleafbookclub for your chance to win prizes by the author!

Made in the USA
Monee, IL
01 December 2020